How the Chipmunk Got Its Stripes

Got Its Stripes

CHARACTERS

Story Woman	Bear
Story Man	Chipmunk
Big Elk	Rabbit
Little Elk	Turtle
Eagle	Morning Birds
Spider	

SETTING

A campfire

Story Woman: Long ago, when the Native Americans still lived in teepees, animals could talk.

Story Man: Big and Little Elk, Eagle, and Spider all told this story, so we know it is true.

Big Elk: We were drinking cool water from the mountain stream. Then we heard a sound in the woods.

Little Elk: The footsteps grew louder and louder.

Big Elk: The earth shook.

Little Elk: The trees trembled. Then we both saw him—

Little Elk and **Big Elk**: BEAR!

Big Elk: We ran away as fast as we could.

Story Woman: The elk knew how strong a bear is.

Eagle: I was flying, looking down at the beautiful valley. I saw the bear chasing the elk. I decided to stay near the clouds.

Story Man: The eagle knew how big a bear is.

Spider: I was almost done weaving my web. Suddenly, Bear stood on his hind legs and said—

Bear: I am Bear! I am big and strong!

Story Woman: And Spider said—

Spider: I know, Bear. And I am small and weak. Do not hurt me, Bear!

Story Woman: And while Bear growled and roared, Spider folded her web and moved on.

Bear: I am the strongest animal in the forest. There is nothing I cannot do!

Story Man: Big Elk, Little Elk, Eagle, and Spider all knew to stay far away from the powerful Bear.

Story Woman: One animal, however, was not so smart.

Story Man: This was a small brown chipmunk. He looked up from his hole in the ground. He wanted to get the better of Bear. He said—

Chipmunk: Bear, do you think you can do anything?

Bear: Yes! Look at me. With one paw I can roll this huge log down the hill.

Story Woman: Mighty Bear pushed the log over. He did not know that a little rabbit lived in the log. The rabbit ran for his life.

Rabbit: My home is gone. Now where shall I hide? Do not hurt me, Bear!

Bear: You see, Chipmunk. I am the strongest animal. All the other animals fear me.

Rabbit: I fear Bear's sharp claws.

Spider: I fear his large jaw and sharp teeth, too.

Little Elk and **Big Elk**: There is nothing Bear cannot do.

Story Man: But Chipmunk had an idea.

Chipmunk: Bear, since you are so big and powerful, can you stop the Sun from rising in the morning?

Bear: I have never tried to stop the Sun from rising. But any animal as big and strong as I am should be able to do that.

Chipmunk: Are you sure?

Bear: Certainly. Tomorrow morning the Sun will not rise. I, Bear, have said so.

Story Woman: As the Sun set in the west, Bear sat down facing the east to wait. When it grew darker, Chipmunk said to Turtle—

Chipmunk: Can you believe how foolish Bear is? He really thinks he can stop the Sun from rising. He may be the strongest animal in the forest, but he is also the most foolish. Just wait and see.

Turtle: Be careful, Chipmunk. Be very careful. No animal likes to be called a fool—least of all strong Bear.

Story Man: That was all Turtle said before going to bed for the night. Soon everything was dark, and all the animals slept.

(*sound of all the animals snoring*)

Story Woman: Before long the east glowed with the light that comes ahead of the Sun. Morning Birds sang.

Morning Birds: Wake up, animals of the forest! A new day is dawning! Time to get up and sing!

Story Man: Bear stared hard at the glowing light in the east.

Bear: Sun, do not rise today. Do not rise!

Story Woman: Despite Bear's words, the Sun rose just as it always had.

Story Man: Bear was very upset. He knew Chipmunk had made a fool of him.

Story Woman: But Chipmunk was pleased. He came out of his hole and ran around in circles, singing—

Chipmunk: The Sun is up! Bear said the Sun would not rise, but it did!

Story Woman: Chipmunk laughed. He laughed so hard he rolled over on his back. The other animals watched as Chipmunk teased Bear.

Chipmunk: Sun is stronger than Bear. Sun is stronger than Bear.

Story Man: Some of the other animals joined in the laughter.

Big Elk: Sharp claws cannot stop the golden Sun from rising.

Eagle: Sharp teeth cannot dim the Sun's bright rays.

Story Woman: But Turtle called out—

Turtle: Beware, animals. If you had Bear's strength, what would you do if you were teased?

Story Woman: Unfortunately, Turtle's warning came too late.

Story Man: Suddenly, Bear lifted his huge paw in the air and pinned Chipmunk to the ground.

Bear: Perhaps I cannot stop the Sun from rising. But you, Chipmunk, shall never see another sunrise!

Story Man: The other animals fled for their lives. Big and Little Elk ran through the dark forest. Eagle flew toward the clouds. Morning Birds found a high tree branch. Spider and Turtle hid in a dead tree trunk.

Bear: Now who is laughing, Chipmunk? I am going to eat you.

Chipmunk: Oh, Bear, oh, oh, oh—you are the strongest, the biggest, the most powerful of all animals! I was only joking.

Bear: I am going to eat you!

Story Woman: Bear did not move his paw.

Chipmunk: Oh, Bear, you are right to be angry with me. I should not have teased you. But please let me say a final prayer before you eat me.

Bear: Say it quickly, Chipmunk. Your time to walk the Sky Road has come!

Chipmunk: I know, Bear, but you are pressing down on me too hard. I can hardly breathe. I can hardly squeak. Please lift your paw a little bit. Then I can say my last prayer. I only need a second to give praise to the one who made wise, powerful Bear and foolish, weak Chipmunk.

Story Man: Bear lifted his huge paw just a tiny bit.

Story Woman: But that tiny bit was enough. Chipmunk squirmed free and ran for his life.

Story Woman: Bear raised his big paw. He was not quite fast enough to catch Chipmunk. However, the tips of his sharp claws scraped along Chipmunk's back. They left three pale scars.

Story Man: To this day, all chipmunks wear those scars as a reminder.

Story Woman: That is what happens when one animal makes a fool of another.

The End